D1180075

This book belongs to:

....

Storybook
Collection

101 Dalmatians and 102 Dalmatians are based on the original book by
Dodie Smith, published by Viking Press.

This is a Parragon book
This edition published in 2005

Parragon
Queen Street House
4 Queen Street
Bath, BA1 1HE, UK

Copyright © 2005 Disney Enterprises, Inc.

All rights reserved. No part of this publication may be reproduced, stored
in a retrieval system or transmitted by any means electronic, mechanical,
photocopying or otherwise without the prior permission of the publisher.

Printed in China
ISBN 1-40546-046-6

Storybook
Collection

p

Contents

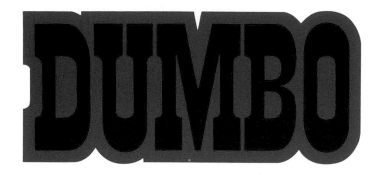

Disney's DUMBO

IF NOT FOR FRIENDS . . .

Dumbo's mother was locked away. Poor little Dumbo felt alone in the world. Without his mother's tender caresses and playful games, he was sad and lonely. The other elephants blamed him for his own mother's imprisonment. They laughed at his big ears and

turned their backs on him when he most needed caring and understanding.

In disbelief, a friendly mouse named Timothy

listened to the mean-spirited gossip of the large elephants.

Knowing that they would be terrified of a little mouse like

him, he decided to give them the fright of their life. After

all, someone had to stick up for little Dumbo. "What was

wrong with having big ears anyway?" thought Timothy.

As far as he was

concerned, Dumbo

was a cute baby

elephant.

So Timothy

waved his arms and

stuck out his

tongue. The elephants shrieked in fear, climbing poles to get away from the small mouse. "Pick on someone your own size!" yelled Timothy.

He chuckled at their silliness. "Imagine being afraid of a small mouse," he laughed. "Wait till I tell the little guy." But Dumbo was scared of Timothy, too. He hid himself in

 a bale of hay and would not come out even for a peanut.

"I'm your friend," Timothy

assured him. He told Dumbo that his ears were special. Then he promised to help him get his mother freed if the little elephant would come out. Hesitantly, Dumbo finally

looked out at his new protector. Deciding to trust Timothy, they went out in search of a miracle.

"We'll make you a star of the circus," suggested Timothy confidently. He came up with a plan. Sneaking into the ringmaster's tent that night, the mouse whispered his great idea to the sleeping man. "Dumbo!" he repeated over and over.

Thinking the idea had come to him in a dream, the ringmaster announced his amazing new act: the smallest

elephant leaping from a springboard to the top of an amazing pyramid of pachyderms!

Dumbo was nervous, but

Timothy encouraged him to try. Running towards the springboard, the little elephant tripped over his ears and fell, knocking over the enormous pyramid and collapsing the tent.

After that, to make matters worse, the ringmaster made Dumbo into a clown. The poor little guy didn't trust the other clowns to keep him safe. They forced him to

jump from a burning building. Dumbo had never been so scared and humiliated! When the show was over, the little elephant was inconsolable.

Timothy tried to comfort his friend. He offered peanuts as he washed the clown paint off with warm, soapy water. Still, Dumbo did not stop crying. Timothy knew that the only one who could help Dumbo now was his mother. So Timothy arranged for a short visit.

Even though only her trunk could hug him, Dumbo basked in his mother's love. Although he was sad to go

back to his tent without her, Dumbo was thankful for Timothy's help.

The next morning, after some strange and restless dreams, the mouse and the elephant awoke high up in a tree. Some crows were laughing as the friends fell into a pond.

"Don't listen to those scarecrows," Timothy told Dumbo, but the elephant was already walking away, head

 down. Everyone was always laughing at him, him and his big ears. Only

Timothy believed they would do great things.

"That's it, Dumbo!" cried his friend. Timothy had been trying to figure out how they had ended up in the tree, when suddenly he realized how special Dumbo's ears really were. The perfect wings! "You can fly!" cheered Timothy.

This news made the crows fall over laughing. "Have you ever seen an elephant fly?" they jeered.

Defending his friend, Timothy yelled at the crows for being so insensitive. "How would you like to be taken away from your mother when you were just a baby and then be sent out into a cold, cruel, heartless world?" he ranted.

The crows apologized. They really hadn't meant any harm.

"What he needs is this magic feather," offered one crow.

Timothy showed his friend: "Look, Dumbo, you can fly!"

Holding the feather in his trunk, Dumbo closed his eyes and flapped his ears. He wanted so much to believe

Timothy! He was flying!

When he opened his eyes again the little elephant was overjoyed. He held the feather tightly, flying through the sky like a bird. Timothy cheered from his seat on

Dumbo's hat while the crows praised the elephant's talent.

It was not long before Timothy's prediction of stardom was a reality. As Dumbo jumped from the burning building again he dropped the magic feather and panicked, but Timothy quickly assured him that he could fly on his own. Restoring his confidence allowed Dumbo to soar, astonishing everyone

who had once made fun of the elephant's big ears.

Finally, Dumbo and his mother were reunited! With love and pride, Timothy signed on as manager for the world's only flying elephant.

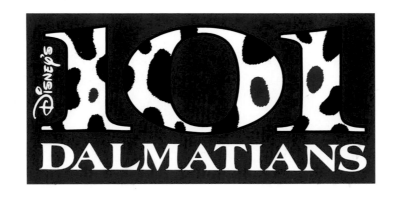

Pongo, Perdita and their fifteen puppies lived in a cozy little house in London. The house belonged to their humans, Roger and Anita. They were perfectly happy until they met Cruella De Vil – Anita's old schoolfriend who simply loved spotted puppies.

She wanted to buy them all and make them into spotted fur coats!

Roger put his foot down. "These puppies are not for sale and that's final."

Cruella was furious but she refused to give up.

One night Cruella's two nasty henchmen, Horace and

Jasper, kidnapped the puppies! Then they drove out to Cruella's old country estate and waited to hear from their boss.

When the puppies got there, they saw lots and lots of other Dalmatian puppies who had also been snatched by Horace and Jasper.

Back at home, Pongo and Perdita could not believe what had happened.

Perdita knew at once that Cruella was behind her missing puppies.

"She has stolen them," sobbed Perdita. "Oh, Pongo, do you think we'll ever find them?"

Pongo knew that the Twilight Bark was their only hope. He would bark his message to the dogs in London.

They would pick it up and pass it along to the dogs in the country. And maybe someone would find the puppies.

That night the Twilight Bark reached a quiet farm where an old English sheepdog known as Colonel lay sleeping peacefully.

"Alert, alert!" shouted Sergeant Tibs, a cat who lived on the farm. "Vital message coming in from London."

The Colonel listened closely. "Fifteen puppies have been stolen!" he cried.

Sergeant Tibs remembered hearing barking at the old De Vil place. They headed straight for the gloomy mansion.

The Colonel helped Tibs look through the window. Sure enough, there were the fifteen puppies – plus their eighty-four new friends!

Tibs and the Colonel overheard Cruella, Jasper and Horace talking. When they heard her plans to make coats out of the puppies, they knew there was no time to waste. The Colonel ran off to get word to Pongo and Perdita while Tibs helped the puppies escape!

As soon as Horace and Jasper realized what was

happening, they tried to stop the puppies. But it was too late. Pongo and Perdita arrived and fought off the foolish thugs as the puppies hurried to safety.

Once all the dogs were safely out of the house, they

thanked the Colonel and Tibs and went on their way. A

black Labrador retriever arranged for them to ride to

London in the back of a removal van that was being

repaired. The dogs waited in a blacksmith's shop.

Suddenly Cruella's big car drove up the street. She

had followed their tracks and was parked and waiting.

But Pongo had a clever idea. There were ashes in the

fireplace. If they all rolled in them, they would be disguised in black soot. Then they could get aboard the van without Cruella

realizing it was them! And that's just what they did.

It worked perfectly until a blob of snow dropped onto a puppy and washed off a patch of soot. From her car, Cruella could see it was a Dalmatian puppy.

"They're escaping!" she cried as the van took off.

There was a
really scary chase.
Cruella tried to pass
the van on the road,
but she ended up
crashing through a
barricade and
driving right into a
huge pile of snow.
Cruella's beautiful
car was a wreck!
And that wasn't all.

She had lost the
puppies! Cruella
threw a tantrum.

Pongo and
Perdita and 99
puppies arrived
home safely, much to
Roger and Anita's
delight. Roger pulled
out a handkerchief

and wiped Pongo's face clean.

"What will we do with all these puppies?" Anita asked.

"We'll keep them," Roger answered. He sat down at the piano and composed a song right on the spot. "We'll buy a big place in the country, and we'll have a plantation," he sang. "A Dalmatian plantation!"

And that's exactly what they did.

Walt Disney's Bambi

One beautiful spring morning a little rabbit named Thumper woke Friend Owl with some wonderful news. A baby deer had been born deep in the woods. "It's happened!" cried the little rabbit. "A new prince is born!"

"What's his name?" asked the animals.

"Why, his name is Bambi," his mother replied.

Soon Bambi met all the other wonderful animals in the forest. First Mrs Quail and her babies stopped to say

hello. Then Mrs Opossum and her family, who liked to hang upside down, smiled at Bambi. Next, a mole poked his head out from the ground to wish Bambi a good day.

Even a flock of little bluebirds flew down to greet the young prince.

Bambi made friends with Thumper and a shy little

skunk called Flower. They laughed and played together every day. Soon, at the pond in the meadow, Bambi made another friend – a playful girl fawn named Faline.

Summer and autumn passed happily for Bambi. And when the winter came, Thumper taught Bambi how to spin and slide on the frozen pond. Bambi had never done anything like this before. "C'mon, it's all right," Thumper told him, gliding across the ice. "The water's stiff!"

Finally winter was over and the spring brought many changes. Bambi had grown into a handsome young buck.

His friends Thumper and Flower had grown up, too. Friend Owl couldn't get over them. He was sure that any moment now they would all meet somebody and become… twitterpated. That meant they would fall in love.

The three friends laughed at the wise old owl and agreed to spend all their time together – until Flower met a lovely girl skunk and got twitterpated. Bambi knew he would miss Flower. But at least he and Thumper could

still spend time together. Then Thumper fell in love, too!

Next it was Bambi's turn. Soon he met a beautiful doe in the meadow. It was his old friend Faline! Bambi suddenly felt dizzy and light as a feather! He was twitterpated. Bambi and Faline frolicked together just as they had done in the meadow when they were young.

But Bambi wasn't the only buck who liked Faline. A stag named Ronno soon pushed his way between them challenging Bambi to a fierce fight. Bambi charged Ronno with all his might and the two bucks butted heads again and again. Finally, Bambi won the fight. And from

that day on, he and Faline were always together.

One autumn morning Bambi smelled something strange – smoke. Just then a majestic stag appeared. It was Bambi's father, the Great Prince. "The forest is on fire!" he cried. "Hurry! We must warn the other animals to run to the river island."

Bambi and the Prince warned all the forest animals.

Then they crossed the river, where they found Faline waiting for them. Bambi and his friends watched as fire destroyed their forest homes and everything around them.

After the fire was out, the old stag turned to Bambi. "I must leave you now," he said. "You will take my place as

Prince of the Forest." Bambi knew this was a great responsibility, but he was ready to accept it.

And Bambi knew that when the last bit of smoke was gone, the animals would bravely rebuild their homes.

Autumn once again turned into winter and winter into spring. The forest was lush and green and smelled of blooming flowers.

Soon Thumper and his little bunnies were waking Friend Owl once again. Faline had given birth to twin fawns. All the animals proudly came to celebrate.

But no one was prouder than Bambi, the new Prince

of the Forest. He stood overlooking the thicket, smiling down on his family, his heart filled with love. Soon, Bambi would teach them the lessons of the forest that he himself had learned so long ago.

Walt Disney's
Lady and the TRAMP

Lady was a happy little dog. She lived in a big house with Jim Dear and Darling. One day Lady learned that Darling was expecting a baby. Lady didn't know that

things in the house would soon be very different.

One day Lady met a scruffy dog named Tramp. Tramp had no home and no family. He went wherever he pleased and did whatever he pleased.

"Believe me," Tramp told Lady and her friends, Jock and Trusty, "babies change everything! Now you'll have nothing but trouble. Just wait and see!"

But Tramp was wrong. When the baby arrived, Lady

had one more wonderful person to care for and love.

Several weeks later, Jim Dear and Darling went off on

a trip. Aunt Sarah came to stay at the house. "Lady," said

Jim Dear, "help Aunt Sarah take care of the baby."

Aunt Sarah brought her Siamese cats with her. They

made a lot of trouble. Lady
barked at the cats, but it
did no good.

"Shame on you, Lady!"
shouted Aunt Sarah.
"Attacking my poor little
angels. A muzzle is what
you need!" She took
Lady right to the pet
shop to buy one.

The muzzle was more than Lady could bear. She had
to run away. When Lady stopped to catch her breath, she

was in a strange part of town surrounded by a pack of mean dogs. Just then her friend Tramp appeared. Seeing that Lady was in danger, he fought the stray dogs and chased them off.

"You poor kid!" said Tramp, looking at the muzzle. He took Lady to the zoo, where a friendly beaver chewed right through the muzzle and freed Lady.

Afterwards, Tramp took Lady to visit one of his favourite places. They shared a romantic dinner for two at Tony's Italian restaurant.

Finally, after a lovely stroll through the park, Lady said, "I must go home. I promised Jim Dear I'd take care of the baby."

"Okay, Pigeon," said Tramp. "But let's have some fun first."

"Tramp, no!" said Lady. But Tramp had already rushed into a nearby yard to chase the squawking chickens.

Suddenly the dogcatcher appeared. Before she knew it, Lady was on her way to the pound without Tramp. Lady was ashamed and scared in the pound – especially when the other dogs began to tease her. A dog named Peg came to Lady's rescue. "Can't you see the poor kid's scared enough already?" Peg said to the other dogs.

The dogs were jealous because Lady had a shiny licence and would soon be going home.

When Lady finally came home, Tramp said, "I'm sorry I got you into trouble, Pidge." But Lady was too angry to listen. She refused to speak to Tramp.

Later that night, Lady saw a rat scurry up a vine to the baby's room. She barked as loudly as she could.

When Tramp heard Lady barking, he came running.

"What's wrong, Pidge?" he asked.

When Lady told him about the rat, Tramp ran into the

house and up the stairs.

Lady pulled at her chain until it broke. Then she ran up to the baby's room to help Tramp fight the rat and save the baby.

"You vicious brutes!" cried Aunt Sarah when she saw Lady and Tramp in the baby's room. "Get away from the baby!"

Aunt Sarah called the dogcatcher to come and take Tramp away.

When Jim Dear and Darling came home that night, Lady helped Jim Dear find the dead rat.

"Lady," said Jim Dear thankfully, "I think you and your friend were trying to save our baby from the rat."

Meanwhile, Jock and Trusty went to find Tramp. They soon caught up with the dogcatcher's wagon. Trusty

began barking very loudly – so loudly, in fact, that he

scared the horses. They reared up and the wagon tipped

over right onto poor Trusty.

Trusty had a broken leg, but he would be just fine.

Lady and Jim Dear arrived just in time to free Tramp.

Jim Dear and Darling were so grateful to Tramp that they asked him to live with them always.

By Christmas of that year, Lady and Tramp had four puppies – and the family's happiness was complete.

Madame Bonfamille and her amazing Aristocats lived in a beautiful house in Paris. There were Marie, Toulouse, Berlioz and Duchess, their mama. The kittens were very talented. Madame loved them very

much and planned to leave her entire fortune to them.

Madame did not keep the fact about her fortune a secret. And her wishes did not make Edgar the butler very happy. So Edgar came up with a plan of his own. He would make the Aristocats disappear so he

could inherit Madame's fortune!

For supper that very evening, Edgar prepared a special dish.

"Come and taste this delicious crème de la crème à la Edgar!" he called.

Unfortunately, it was very delicious. The Aristocats and their friend Roquefort the

mouse ate it all. They soon fell fast asleep.

Following his plan, Edgar put them in a basket and

drove them out into the country. He soon met two noisy

dogs who loved to chase anything on wheels. Edgar lost control of his motorcycle and drove right into a river.

The basket holding the Aristocats fell off the motorcycle and under a bridge. When the cats awoke,

they did not know where they were. How would they find their way home?

Soon Thomas O'Malley, the alley cat, found the Aristocats and offered his help. He was quite taken with Duchess.

O'Malley arranged a ride aboard a milk van. But the cats were discovered and chased off the van.

Concerned for their safety, O'Malley decided to accompany the Aristocats back to Paris. After the very long walk, O'Malley convinced Duchess to stop at his place and rest before going home to Madame.

But when they got to O'Malley's place, his jazz-playing

friends were singing and dancing up a storm. And the Aristocats wanted to meet them all, especially Scat Cat. The kittens joined in the fun, but soon it was time to go home. O'Malley tried to talk Duchess into staying with him, but she was too worried about Madame.

O'Malley agreed to take the Aristocats home. He no sooner saw them to their door when Roquefort came running after him. "Duchess needs help!" cried the little mouse. "Come quickly!"

When Edgar saw the Aristocats, he grabbed them and stuffed them inside a pillowcase. Then he hid them in the oven while he pulled out a huge trunk stamped

"Timbuktu".

O'Malley sent Roquefort to get Scat Cat and his friends and bring them to Madame's. Then he ran back to the house to help Duchess. He cornered Edgar in the barn and there was a terrible fight.

Edgar pinned poor O'Malley to the wall with a pitchfork!

Suddenly Scat Cat and his friends were at the barn

door. They managed to overpower Edgar. As Roquefort

popped open the trunk to let the Aristocats out, the

animals made sure
that Edgar took their
place inside. A few
minutes later, some
men came to pick up
the trunk headed for
Timbuktu.

There was the
happiest of reunions
with Madame! She
could not believe her precious cats were home safe and
sound. And Madame had Thomas O'Malley and his

friends to thank for it.

Madame could see that O'Malley and Duchess were in love. She invited him to live with them. Now her family was complete. And as for O'Malley's musician friends, Madame threw a great party and invited them all to play!

THE
LION KING

Everything in the animal kingdom had its place in the circle of life. When the Lion King, Mufasa, and his queen, Sarabi, had a cub named Simba, Mufasa knew that one day Simba would be king. Everyone bowed in respect as Rafiki the baboon introduced the young prince to all the animals.

Only one lion – Mufasa's brother, Scar – refused to attend the ceremony. He was not happy that Simba would be next in line for Mufasa's throne.

But Simba grew into a happy, healthy cub. One day he proudly told his uncle, "Someday I'm going to rule the whole kingdom! Everything except that shadowy place.

I'm not allowed to go there."

"You're absolutely right, Simba," his uncle agreed slyly.

"Only the bravest lions can go to the elephant graveyard."

Scar deliberately tempted his adventurous nephew.

Simba immediately raced home and convinced his

friend Nala to explore the elephant graveyard. It was

creepier than they ever imagined.

Zazu, Mufasa's adviser, caught up with the cubs and

warned them it was dangerous, too.

But Simba only laughed at Zazu. Then he heard

someone laughing

back. He turned to

see three enemy

hyenas ready for

lunch. "He's a king

fit for a meal,"

laughed one.

The nasty hyenas

chased the cubs right into a trap. Suddenly there was a tremendous roar. Mufasa arrived and frightened the hyenas away.

Simba was very proud of his father. "We'll always be

together, right?" he asked Mufasa later that evening.

"Look up at the stars, Simba," said Mufasa. "Those are the great kings of the past looking

down on us.
Remember those
kings will always be
there to guide you. So
will I."

Although Scar was
very angry with the
hyenas for letting

Simba escape, he made a bargain with them. If they

helped him become king, they could have their run of the

Pride Lands. And Scar had a plan.

Later Scar brought Simba to a gorge and promised

him a wonderful surprise if he would wait on a certain

rock. Then he signalled to the hyenas.

The surprise was a stampeding herd of wildebeests!

The earth trembled as the wildebeests headed right

into the gorge and straight towards Simba. Simba

held onto a tree

branch but was

slipping fast.

In an instant

Mufasa appeared

and grabbed his

son. He got Simba

to safety, but then he slipped off the ledge and fell into the thundering stampede.

When everything was quiet once more, Simba found his father lying lifeless at the foot of a cliff. Simba had not seen Scar push Mufasa to his death. Simba believed it was all his fault.

"Run away, Simba," Scar advised the young cub. "Run away and never return."

Scar watched as the young cub ran away, chased by

the hyenas. Then Scar returned to Pride Rock and announced to the lions that he would be their new king.

Simba ended up in the desert, where he collapsed from heat and exhaustion. Luckily two curious creatures found him – a meerkat called Timon and a warthog named Pumbaa.

Simba's new friends took him home to the jungle, where they introduced him to Timon's idea of hakuna matata – "no worries".

Simba tried to put the past behind him, but it was difficult. One day a young lioness appeared, looking for help. It was Nala. She told Simba the sad story of what had happened since Scar had taken over the Pride Lands.

But Simba could not face going back — at least not until Rafiki appeared and led him to a vision of his father. "You are my son and the one true king. You must take your place in the circle of life," Mufasa explained.

So Simba returned to the Pride Lands with his friends by his side. There was a great battle. Finally, Scar

cornered Simba and confessed what he had done many years ago. "You didn't kill your father," Scar said evilly. "I did."

At last Simba found the strength to fight back. He flipped the evil lion right over the edge of the rock into the jaws of the waiting hyenas.

When the fighting was over, Simba took his rightful place as king and restored the Pride Lands to a place of peace. And when Simba's and Nala's little cub was born, a brand-new circle of life was begun.

Walt Disney's THE JUNGLE BOOK

Long ago, deep in the jungles of faraway India, there lived a wise black panther named Bagheera. One day, as Bagheera sat in a tree, he saw something surprising. "Why, it's a Man-cub!" said the panther.

Bagheera was not able to care for the Man-cub, so he took the baby to live with a family of wolves.

The wolves named the little boy Mowgli and raised him as one of their own.

Ten rainy seasons came and went. Mowgli grew, and no Man-cub was happier than he. The creatures of the jungle were good to him.

But one jungle animal did not wish Mowgli well. It was Shere Khan, the strong and cunning tiger.

Shere Khan feared nothing but Man's gun and Man's fire. He was sure the Man-cub would grow up to be a hunter.

"Shere Khan has returned to our part of the jungle!" Akela the wolf said one day. "Surely he will try to kill the boy." Mowgli was no longer safe.

"It is time for Mowgli to return to his own kind," Bagheera said. "I will take him to the Man village."

"Hurry," Akela said. "There is no time to lose."

Bagheera and Mowgli started on their way.

"We'll spend the night here," Bagheera said as they settled down on the branch of a tree.

Just then Kaa the snake appeared. He thought Mowgli would make a tasty morsel. The snake used his hypnotic eyes to put Mowgli in a trance. He wrapped the Man-cub in his coils.

Bagheera awoke just in time to smack Kaa on the head

and send him on his way. It was time to keep moving!

Mowgli decided he didn't want to go with Bagheera. "The jungle is my home!" the Man-cub insisted. He went off on his own.

Along the way Mowgli saw a parade of elephants. He thought it was wonderful and wanted to march along with them. But when it was time for the elephant inspection, Colonel Hathi took a closer look at Mowgli.

"What happened to your trunk?" asked the Colonel.

"Why – you're a Man-cub!" he cried.

Bagheera came to Mowgli's rescue. He insisted on

taking him to the Man village, but Mowgli refused once

more. "Then from now on, you're on your own!" Bagheera told him.

Mowgli soon met a good-natured bear named Baloo. Baloo helped Mowgli forget his troubles. They played together, swam together and ate sweet, ripe bananas and coconuts all day long.

As the two friends floated on the river, a group of monkeys swooped down on Mowgli. They picked him up and dragged him off to the ancient city of the monkey king.

The monkey king wanted
something from Mowgli.
"Teach me the secret
of fire," King Louie
demanded. "Then
I can be human
like you!"

Bagheera and
Baloo arrived in time
to help Mowgli escape from the monkeys. "Now you see
why you must leave the jungle!" they pleaded.

But Mowgli still did not believe his friends. He ran away

from them again – right into the great Shere Khan himself.

"I'm not afraid of you, Shere Khan!" said Mowgli bravely. A storm began to blow around them. Suddenly a bolt of lightning struck nearby.

The lightning started a small fire. Mowgli grabbed a burning branch and tied it to Shere Khan's tail. The terrified tiger ran away, never to be seen again.

As Mowgli proudly walked through the jungle with his friends, he heard a new and beautiful sound. It was a girl from the Man village, singing a sweet song.

Mowgli couldn't look away. He stopped walking to listen. "Go on, Mowgli!" Bagheera urged. "Go on!"

Mowgli knew that he must follow the girl and her song. She smiled at Mowgli as he walked with her all the way to the village. He turned to wave goodbye to his friends.

Baloo and Bagheera watched Mowgli leave. Their hearts were sad, but they knew it was as it should be. Their Man-cub had found his true home at last.

GOING TO THE DOGS

After spending three years in prison for stealing ninety-nine Dalmatian puppies, Cruella De Vil was free. She had been able to convince the judge that she now loved dogs. But the judge had one warning for Cruella: if she repeated her crime, he would take away her freedom *and* her fortune!

As Cruella exited the prison, her ever faithful valet, Alonso, greeted her with a gift – a hairless dog.

"I think I'll call him Fluffy," Cruella announced, delighted.

Across town, Kevin Shepherd ran the Second Chance Dog Shelter. Kevin really loved dogs.

He was playing tug-of-war with a dog named Drooler, while the other dogs and Waddlesworth – a macaw who thought he was a dog – looked on.

But life at Second Chance was not all fun and games. The rent had not been paid, and the landlord was threatening to evict Kevin and the dogs.

"You and your mangy pack are out of here tomorrow!" the landlord shouted.

Kevin didn't know what to do.

The next day, the landlord came back to kick Kevin out. But Cruella heard about the situation and decided to buy the place! She transformed the Second Chance Dog Shelter into a palace. The dogs were even given bubble baths and new hairstyles.

But Chloe Simon, Cruella's probation officer, was not so sure

Cruella was cured. In fact, Cruella had tried to make Chloe's own dog Dipstick into a fur coat a few years ago!

More recently, Chloe's Dalmatians, Dottie and Dipstick, had become  proud parents of puppies. Their names were Domino, Little Dipper and Oddball.

Chloe brought her dogs to work on the same day that Cruella came in for a visit. While Chloe talked to Cruella, one of the puppies got into trouble. Oddball, who didn't have spots yet, saw the copier repairman covered in ink spots. She raced over to get some of her own. But after Oddball rolled around in the ink, the repairman accidentally knocked her out of the window!

It was Cruella who first looked out of the window and spotted Oddball. She also saw the two other puppies, who had gone out to try to rescue her!

Chloe rushed to the window. One by one, she was able to pull the puppies safely back into the room.

Just then, Big Ben, the famous London clock, began to chime. It had a strange effect on Cruella. Her old dog-hating, fur-loving nature was returning!

Everywhere she looked she saw spots! She ran into the street, shouting, "Cruella's ba-a-a-ck! Ha-ha-ha-ha!"

Cruella ran home and found a design for a hooded Dalmatian puppy coat that she had sketched years ago. Then she sent Alonso out to steal 102 Dalmatian puppies while she went to visit the furrier Jean-Pierre LePelt. Together they plotted to create the spotted coat.

Meanwhile, Chloe and Kevin happened to meet up in the park. They were enjoying a puppet show along

with their pets, when Oddball got entangled in some balloon strings and started floating away. Luckily, Kevin was able to grab the balloons and rescue Oddball.

Later on, Kevin and Chloe went out on a date. Waddlesworth came along and brought Oddball a spotted sweater.

Chloe liked Kevin, but she couldn't understand why he trusted Cruella. Kevin explained that Cruella had every reason to be good: if she was ever cruel to an animal again, the judge would give all her money to the Second Chance Animal Shelter!

The next day, the police came to Kevin's shelter, looking for stolen Dalmatian puppies. They searched and found a sackful of puppies. Then Chloe and Cruella  arrived. Cruella accused Kevin of setting her up to get her money. But, in fact, Cruella had set Kevin up! She wanted to make sure someone else took the blame for her crime. Kevin and his pets were taken to jail!

That evening, Cruella invited Chloe and Dipstick to a fancy party at her mansion. Cruella welcomed them and asked, "Are your little spotted puppies safe and snug at home?" Little did Chloe know that Cruella had sent LePelt to steal Dipstick's and Dottie's puppies!

Then Dipstick heard a tiny bark. Cruella's dog

Fluffy was beckoning to him. He and Chloe followed

Fluffy to Cruella's fur room. There Chloe discovered

the design for the Dalmatian puppy coat. Just then

Cruella appeared – and locked Chloe in the room! But

Dipstick escaped and raced home.

At Chloe's house, LePelt was struggling to get the dogs into a sack. Oddball sounded the Twilight Bark just before LePelt captured her. Soon dogs all over London were barking the alarm. Dipstick arrived home just as LePelt was driving

off. Bravely, he leaped inside the lorry that was carrying his family away.

In prison, Kevin and his pets also heard the Twilight Bark. "We have to get out of here!" Kevin said.

Waddlesworth waddled over to the guard and stole his keys. Then he set Kevin and the others free!

Back at Cruella's house, Fluffy helped Chloe escape, too.

At the same time, Kevin and Chloe arrived at Chloe's apartment to find the dogs were gone! But Drooler found a clue – a train ticket. Cruella and LePelt would be on the 10 P.M. Orient Express to Paris! Kevin, Chloe and the pets raced across town to the train station.

When they arrived, they saw Oddball racing

alongside the departing Orient Express. She had got

away from Cruella, but

was trying to hop aboard

the train to save her

family.

Waddlesworth, who

never thought he could

fly, now realized he *had*

to. Flapping his wings furiously, he flew to Oddball,

lifted her up and dropped her safely on the train.

In Paris, Cruella and LePelt drove the puppies to LePelt's workshop where Alonso locked them in the cellar. Oddball and Waddlesworth had been hiding in the backseat, unnoticed. They sneaked into the workshop, and Waddlesworth began tearing at  a hole leading into the cellar. If he could make the hole big enough, all of the puppies could escape!

Meanwhile, through the Twilight Bark, Kevin and Chloe realized the puppies were in LePelt's workshop.

But just as they arrived and opened the cellar door, Cruella came up from behind and locked them inside! They were trapped – but now the hole that Waddlesworth had been working on was large enough for the puppies to crawl through and get away!

Just then, Cruella saw Oddball leading the puppies up the stairs and out of the window! Enraged, she raced after them across a narrow bridge and into the bakery next door.

Cruella did her best to get the puppies, but she had no chance against the 102 Dalmatians. In the end, Cruella was baked into a cake – icing and all. The police took Cruella away. The puppies were safe and sound!

Several days later, Alonso arrived at Second Chance Dog Shelter with a cheque for the amount of Cruella's entire estate. The judge had kept his promise. All of Cruella's money would go to the dogs.

As the celebrating began, Chloe suddenly noticed something. "Oddball's got her spots!" she cried, pointing to the little puppy. No more spotted sweaters for Oddball. She finally had the real thing!

One of the Pack

Rules, rules, rules. Scamp hated rules. Lady's and Tramp's other puppies were obedient and good. But Scamp liked to play. And sometimes, when Scamp played, he forgot about the rules. He tracked mud into the house and chewed on Jim Dear's hats.

So one night, Jim Dear decided that Scamp had to sleep outside, chained to

the kennel. Tramp tried to explain to his son that being part of a family meant following certain rules.

"But I want to run wild and free – like a real dog!" Scamp replied.

Later, Scamp heard dogs howling on the other side of the fence. He peeked through the gate and watched as a group of street dogs outwitted a dogcatcher. They were so wild! Scamp wanted to join them, but his chain held him back. The dogs ran off.

Then, as Scamp dreamed about life without fences or leashes, it happened. He pulled against the chain, and it broke loose from his collar! Scamp was free!

"Hey, you guys!" Scamp shouted after the street dogs. "Wait for me!"

Scamp ran through the dark streets, looking for the dogs. He caught up with one of them, Angel, in a dark alley. "Listen," Angel said to Scamp, "you don't belong on the street."

Scamp wouldn't listen. He followed Angel to the junkyard, the dogs' hangout. There he met Buster, the rough and tough leader of the Junkyard Dogs. Buster agreed to let Scamp be one of them . . . if Scamp could pass a test of courage.

It wouldn't be easy. Scamp had to fetch a tin can

from the paws of a sleeping dog – a mean, vicious dog

named Reggie. Scamp managed to slide the tin free

and was tiptoeing away when – *clang!* – he ran right

into a dustbin. Reggie awoke with a snarl.

In a flash, Reggie was after Scamp. Somehow, Angel accidentally ended up in the middle of the chase. She fled around a corner – and right into the path of the dogcatcher's van. The dogcatcher scooped Angel up in his net.

Scamp had to save her! He leaped and grabbed onto the long handle of the net with his teeth. The van swerved. Reggie ran out into the road and *crash!* The van knocked Reggie into a fruit stand. The dogcatcher nabbed Reggie, but Scamp and Angel got away.

Scamp got the tin *and* saved Angel! But Buster still wasn't convinced that Scamp was ready to be a Junkyard Dog. He still had one more test for Scamp.

Then, Scamp and Angel went for a stroll around town. They chased fireflies. They shared a plate of spaghetti outside Tony's restaurant. It was a real case of puppy love.

Later, while chasing a squirrel, Scamp and Angel ended up on Jim Dear's and Darling's street. Jim Dear was out with Tramp and Lady, looking for Scamp. Scamp and Angel hid as they went by.

"C'mon, Tramp," Jim Dear was saying. "We'll find Scamp tomorrow." The three went home.

"The Tramp is your father?" Angel whispered to Scamp. She told him that Tramp was a legend among street dogs. Scamp couldn't believe it. His dad had once been a Junkyard Dog?

Scamp and Angel crept up to the house and peeked through the window. Scamp was surprised by how sad his family looked. He didn't think they'd miss him so much.

"I can't believe you'd run away from a home like this!" Angel said to him. She desperately wanted a family of her own. But Scamp still wanted to be wild and free. One more test to pass – and he'd be a Junkyard Dog.

That test came the next day at the big Fourth of July picnic. Jim Dear and Darling were there with Aunt Sarah, Lady, Tramp and the other pups. Buster dared Scamp to steal some chicken from his own family's picnic! Scamp didn't want to, but he did it, anyway.

Tramp chased after Scamp and tried to talk him into coming home. But Scamp said no. Tramp was crushed, but he told his son, "When you've had enough, our door's always open."

Then, since Scamp had passed his final test, Buster took off Scamp's collar. He was now a real Junkyard Dog – wild and free.

But Scamp's freedom did not last very long. That very same night, Buster betrayed him! He set Scamp up to be nabbed by the dogcatcher. "Well, look here. No collar," said the dogcatcher. Scamp was going straight to the pound.

Scamp was cold, alone and afraid. He realized he had turned his back on his own family for a scoundrel like Buster. "I wish I were home," said Scamp to himself.

Luckily, Angel spotted Scamp in the back of the

dogcatcher's van. She raced to Jim Dear's and Darling's house and found Tramp. "Hurry!" she said. "Scamp's in trouble!"

Meanwhile,
at the pound,
Scamp was
thrown into a
cage with . . .
Reggie!

Reggie had just grabbed hold of the pup when Tramp

burst through the door. With a few old street-dog moves,

Tramp rescued Scamp from Reggie *and* the pound.

"I'm so sorry," Scamp said to his dad. "I shouldn't

have run away."

Tramp took Scamp and Angel home with him. Scamp's family was so happy to see him . . . and his new friend. "Oh, she's a little Angel!" said Darling. They were one big happy family again – with one very happy new member.

As for Scamp, he still didn't like his baths. But it sure was good to be home.

The End